THE SKELETON SECRET
AN UNOFFICIAL MINECRAFTER MYSTERIES SERIES
BOOK THREE

THE SKELETON SECRET
AN UNOFFICIAL MINECRAFTER MYSTERIES SERIES
BOOK THREE

Winter Morgan

Sky Pony Press
New York

Copyright © 2018 by Hollan Publishing, Inc.

Minecraft® is a registered trademark of Notch Development AB.

The Minecraft game is copyright © Mojang AB.

Sky Pony Press books may be purchased in bulk at special discounts for sales promotion, corporate gifts, fund-raising, or educational purposes. Special editions can also be created to specifications. For details, contact the Special Sales Department, Sky Pony Press, 307 West 36th Street, 11th Floor, New York, NY 10018 or info@skyhorsepublishing.com.

Sky Pony® is a registered trademark of Skyhorse Publishing, Inc.®, a Delaware corporation.

Minecraft® is a registered trademark of Notch Development AB.
The Minecraft game is copyright © Mojang AB.

Visit our website at www.skyponypress.com.

10 9 8 7 6 5 4 3 2 1

Library of Congress Cataloging-in-Publication Data is available on file.

Cover design by Brian Peterson
Cover photo by Megan Millar

Print ISBN: 978-1-5107-3189-9
Ebook ISBN: 978-1-5107-3195-0

Printed in Canada

TABLE OF CONTENTS

THE SKELETON SECRET

PRACTICE MAKES PERFECT

Edison's brewing station was covered in fermented spider eyes, Nether wart, glowstone dust, and a myriad of ingredients used to craft potions. His brown hair fell in his face, his gray T-shirt was stained with various potions, and his black sneakers were hurting him because he had been standing so long. For the last two days, he had been consumed with brewing countless batches of the potion of invisibility. Once Edison was finished brewing, Billy would measure how long the potion lasted.

"I was invisible for more than five minutes, right?" asked Edison.

"No, it was two minutes." He showed Edison the watch.

"Seriously?" Edison was irritated at himself. He thought he was a better alchemist than that. "I'm never going to win a medal."

"I think you'll win," said Billy.

"Not with a potion that lasts only two minutes. I need to be invisible for much longer."

"Well, try to brew another batch. I'll time you again." Billy, dressed in his usual khaki shorts and a blue button-down shirt, looked down at the stopwatch.

"Okay, and this time I hope I stay invisible for much longer," Edison remarked.

He had to perfect his ability to brew quickly while not letting the swiftness of the process sacrifice the quality of the potion. If the potion was too weak, he'd lose the contest. His house was a mess because he had done nothing but brew for the past few weeks. Edison was putting a lot of effort into getting ready for this renowned competition. He admitted that he wanted to win first place, but he knew that there would be many alchemists from all around the Overworld at the competition, and some were incredibly fast at brewing. Edison tried to brew his potions quickly, but he felt as if the more he practiced, the worse he became at brewing. It didn't make any sense.

"After all the time I've spent practicing, shouldn't I be getting better at brewing? I feel like I'm getting worse, and I don't understand why. I am trying my hardest," Edison wondered aloud.

"I think you are working too hard and you're exhausted, and it's slowing you down. You need a break," suggested Billy as pushed his wavy blond hair from his eyes.

"A break? I don't have time for a break!" Edison

dropped another fermented spider eye into a potion of night vision, which resulted in a fresh batch of the potion of invisibility. He took a sip. "Time me now," he said.

Billy timed Edison, but he was distracted when he saw someone appear at the door. He opened it.

"Amira! Omar!" He was excited to see his old friends.

Amira and Omar walked into Edison's house juggling water bottles in their arms, trying not to drop them as they made their way to the brewing station.

"You're back!" Billy exclaimed.

"Where's Edison?" asked Omar.

"He's here. He's just invisible," Billy said. "He's practicing for the brewing competition, but I think he's overdoing it. He's consumed with this competition. I think he needs to take a break."

"Just because I'm invisible doesn't mean that I can't hear you, Billy," Edison warned.

Edison's potion wore off, and he reappeared by the brewing station.

"You're back!" Edison exclaimed. His friends had been away for a month and he had missed them, but that didn't stop him from asking, "Billy, did you time how long I was invisible?"

Billy fumbled with his stopwatch. "I'm sorry, I was distracted. I was just so happy to see our old friends."

"No need to apologize." Edison smiled. "I'll brew another batch, and you can time me later." He walked over to his friends. "What are you doing back here?"

"We told you we'd come back to Farmer's Bay for your brewing competition," said Amira.

"Really? Just for me? The competition is no big deal. You shouldn't have traveled all the way back here."

"No *big* deal!" Billy raised his voice and sighed. "You've been obsessing about this competition forever."

"Okay." Edison looked at the floor as he spoke, his cheeks were red, and he was embarrassed. "It's a big deal. I'm honored you came back to watch me. I'm just worried you're going to see me lose."

Amira said, "We are so happy you're in the competition. It's such an honor. You should really just have fun during the brewing event and not stress over winning and losing."

"And we brought you a present." Omar pointed to the many bottles on Edison's brewing stand.

Edison counted the bottles. "Wow, this is great. I can't believe you brought me all these bottles. How did you know I was running low on them?"

"Good guess," said Omar.

"We did a lot of fishing when we were on our trip, and we kept pulling in bottles. We thought they'd be helpful to have in the competition," said Amira.

"Thank you. These are incredibly helpful," said Edison as he looked at the bottles. "You have to tell us about your trip. Did you return most of the stolen treasures?"

"Not all of it, but a lot." Omar listed the various places he had visited with Amira. "And we searched for all the people who had their treasure stolen. They were so excited to get it back, which was very nice to see. Yet I just couldn't get used to a life at sea. I missed Farmer's Bay."

"Does this mean you're going to stay in Farmer's Bay?" asked Billy.

"Yes," Omar replied. "When the brewing competition organizers found out I was coming here to see you, they asked if I could build the stage for the brewing competition. After I finish that I am going to design another building for Dante. He wants a large beach house on the shores of Farmer's Bay. I'm going to build it and when I'm done, I'll stay here. "

"Wow, you're going to build the stage. That's so cool." Edison was excited to imagine standing on the stage that Omar built. He was also pleased that the competition would take place in the neighboring town of Verdant Valley, which gave him more time to prepare for the competition.

"Yes, I am supposed to start work on it tomorrow, and then I get to build a beach house here," Omar replied.

"That sounds nice." Edison thought about the grand structure Omar would build. Since Omar had completed Dante's castle last month, Dante had invited everyone over multiple times for parties. He could only imagine the events they'd attend at the new beach house. Edison was also thrilled to have his old friend Omar back in town.

"What about you, Amira?" asked Billy.

"I will help Omar build the beach house, but then

I'm going back to my life at sea. Dante is going to help me deliver the remaining stolen goods. But we aren't here to talk about us. We're here to celebrate you. How can we help you prepare for the contest?"

Edison looked at all of the bottles lined up on his brewing stand. "I think you've both done enough. I'm so glad that you replenished my supply of bottles."

"Well, if you can think of anything else that might help you, let us know," said Amira.

"We're off to see Dante." Omar excused himself, and Amira followed him.

Billy looked down at the stopwatch. "Should I time you again? This time I promise to pay attention."

Edison put another fermented spider eye into his last batch of potion of night vision and swallowed. Billy stared at the stopwatch. "Wow," Billy called out gleefully, "you've surpassed the last time you were invisible. This is a very strong potion."

"Great!" Edison was thrilled that he was finally making progress.

A thunderous noise boomed throughout the town. Billy looked over to see someone ripping Edison's door from the hinges. "It looks like zombies are trying to get into your house. Edison, where are you?"

There was no response.

2

SKELETON INVASION

"Edison!" Billy's voice cracked. "I need help!"
There was no reply, just the sound of the door crashing to the ground as four vacant-eyed zombies stomped over the broken door and lunged at Billy.

Billy barely had enough time to grab his diamond armor and pull an enchanted diamond sword from his inventory. He adjusted the armor, swung at the zombies, and called for Edison one last time.

"Billy?" Edison reappeared by the brewing stand, extremely groggy, his gray T-shirt covered in sweat, and his brown hair a mess. He rubbed his eyes and tried to process the battle that was occurring in his small living room. Billy had slain one zombie, but the remaining three undead beasts now surrounded him.

"Help!" Billy called out while slashing his sword into a zombie that fell against the emerald design on Edison's wall.

Edison gulped a potion of strength, grabbed as many bottles of potions that could harm zombies as he could, and splashed the smelly creatures. With one splash, two of the zombies were destroyed. Billy struck the final zombie.

"Where were you?" asked Billy.

Edison was confused. "What are you talking about? I was invisible and then the potion wore off."

"Didn't you hear me call out to you?" asked Billy.

"No." Edison paused. "When did you do that?"

"When you were invisible."

"That's strange," Edison said. "I didn't hear you call for help."

"I don't think that potion makes you invisible. I believe it makes you disappear."

Edison laughed and replied, "No way." He looked down at his door. "I have to repair this. When did the zombies rip it off?"

"When you were supposedly invisible," remarked Billy, but he didn't have time to debate his best friend because an arrow shot through the open doorway, piercing Billy's unarmored arm and weakening him.

"Take this." Edison tried to hand Billy a cup of milk, but Billy couldn't reach for it. A barrage of arrows flew through the door, landing in Billy's arm. He cried out in pain and disappeared.

Edison put the milk back in his inventory and raced outside to battle the skeleton army that was stationed in front of his house. When he sprinted out the door, he saw Erin and Peyton in the middle of a fierce fight with the skeletons. Omar and Amira rushed from the shoreline to help them battle the bony beasts. Edison leaped at a skeleton, striking it with his sword.

"Use your potions!" instructed Omar.

Edison pulled out bottles of potion and doused every skeleton in his sight. One by one the skeletons lost hearts, and he watched his friends defeat the lanky creatures as the sound of rattling bones, rain, and thunder swirled around in his head. He was feeling woozy, and he wasn't sure if it was due to the exhaustion of this impromptu battle or if it was from the potion he had brewed. It was very strong, and he was concerned that he'd missed seeing the skeletons break down his door. He didn't remember anything. He'd never had a reaction like this before, and it worried him. What would happen if he disappeared during the competition? Edison wanted to get back to his brewing stand and experiment with the potion while Billy stood watch, but the rain was pouring down and more skeletons were spawning every second.

"When is this rain going to stop?" Edison asked nobody in particular. It was a rhetorical question. Nobody knew the answer.

"Edison!" Billy cried. "I'm outnumbered!"

Edison splashed potions on the skeletons that were inches from Billy as he dashed from his home. "Oh no," Edison exclaimed. "I only have one bottle left."

"Seriously?" Erin questioned as she tried to catch her breath. She only had two hearts left, and she knew if it didn't stop raining soon, she'd be destroyed.

Another thunderous boom shook the wet, muddy ground at Farmer's Bay as the sound of clanging bones grew louder.

"Oh my!" Omar's jaw dropped.

A single-file line of skeletons walked down the muddy path toward the gang. With no potions left, the gang had to rely on their sword-fighting skills. They tried to come up with a quick battle plan. Erin asked Peyton, a first-rate archer, to use her bow and arrow to strike the skeletons. She told Edison he should brew some more potions.

"I can't do it now." Edison pointed to his house. "I have no door. I won't be able to brew potions while skeletons are shooting arrows at me."

The skeletons were almost upon them, but the gang collectively leaped at the bony beasts while trying to shelter themselves from the arrows that flew through the rain. A bolt of lightning lit up the sky, but it didn't strike any of the skeletons.

"When is it going to stop raining?" Billy cried as he was destroyed for the second time.

After respawning, Billy drank a cup of milk to replenish his energy and get ready for this never-ending battle. He clutched his diamond sword as he ran back to his friends.

As the gang battled the skeletal mob with arrows and swords, a man with red hair and wearing a black jacket rushed toward them and joined in the battle against the skeletons.

"When is it going to stop raining?" Peyton looked up at the sky.

Coincidentally as Peyton uttered those words, the rain stopped, but it was dusk, and the skeletons remained. "What is going on?" she questioned.

"I can explain," the man in the black jacket replied.

"Who are you?" asked Edison. He was annoyed because he didn't want to get sidetracked with a new-comer and a possible mystery to solve when he was just a week away from his brewing competition.

"I'm—" the redheaded man started to say, but two arrows ripped into his arm and destroyed him.

The gang battled the skeletons, but as they destroyed one skeleton, a new one would spawn and simply replace the one they had defeated.

"This is an impossible battle," Peyton complained.

"But we have no choice." Erin slew a skeleton and said, "We have to destroy them." She reached down and picked up a dropped bone from the muddy ground.

"It seems like they're not going to stop spawning. We can't fight them all night. We'll run out of sup-plies," Omar rationalized.

"I've never seen anything like this in my life." Edison looked out at a second army of skeletons marching into Farmer's Bay.

"No, you haven't," the redheaded stranger said as he reappeared in front of them.

3
BACKSTORY

"Tell us who you are," Edison demanded. He wanted an answer before the skeletons destroyed this peculiar stranger with messy red hair and a black jacket.

"I'm Wayne," the stranger replied while slamming his sword against a skeleton.

"What do you know about this skeleton invasion?" questioned Peyton.

"This same skeleton invasion happened in my town, and ever since we were invaded, I've been tracking down the culprit behind these attacks."

"Really? How long have you been following him?" asked Edison.

"A few months. It's not easy, because I'm doing it on my own," declared Wayne as he swiped a skeleton's arm bone, weakening the beast. Edison hit the weakened skeleton, obliterating it.

"Who is this person?" While these words fell from Edison's lips, he could feel himself getting back into detective mode.

"I don't know his name," Wayne replied, "but I can tell you that he's very tricky."

"How?" Erin wanted more details.

"He works quickly, and he knows what he's doing. Or maybe I'm just not good at stopping him. I haven't figured that out yet," confessed Wayne.

"Well, we're not going to let his skeletons invade Farmer's Bay," Billy said defiantly.

"What can you tell us about this criminal?" Edison was beginning to collect facts, which he needed in order to solve the case.

"I've learned that he has a system." Wayne spoke loudly. He wanted to make sure everyone heard him while they were in the midst of the intense skeleton battle. Every few minutes he'd pause to catch his breath. Eventually he was able to tell the entire story. "He creates a spawner in a cave outside of the town and then terrorizes the town with nonstop skeleton attacks until everyone is so weak that they surrender all of their goods. This has been going on for a very long time, and he has to be stopped. He ransacked the jungle where I live. It's been months, and we haven't recovered. I promised the townspeople I'd find him and stop him, but he's a hard person to corner."

The gang was upset that their town was under attack, but Edison was particularly upset. He knew he had to help his town, and he wouldn't be able to prepare for the competition. However, he said, "I will help you find this person and end this pointless battle. He won't steal from us."

"Me too!" added Billy.

The others joined in. Each time someone said they'd help, Wayne became more energized and slew more skeletons. Despite more bony beasts spawning, there was a positive energy among the group.

"Do you know where the spawner is now?" asked Edison.

"No," Wayne said. "I didn't even know you guys were under attack until I saw the skeletons. I was just walking over from Verdant Valley. My friend Anna told me there was an alchemist here, and I wanted to buy some potions. Then it started to rain, and I spotted the skeletons. Once the rain stopped and they continued to spawn at such a fast rate, I knew he was behind it."

"Anna?" asked Billy. "Does she have purple hair and wear ripped jeans and a plaid red shirt?"

"Yes," replied Wayne.

"Anna's our friend!" exclaimed Billy as he struck what felt like the millionth skeleton he battled that day.

"I'm the alchemist," said Edison, "but I'm running low on potions, so I can't sell you any."

"That's a shame," Wayne responded while annihilating four skeletons.

"Wow, you're an excellent fighter," marveled Omar.

"I've been battling skeletons for months. It's a skill I acquired but wish I didn't have. I'd much rather be in the jungle where I live," said Wayne as he slew two more skeletons.

"How are we going to battle all of these skeletons?" asked Amira. "We have to find the spawner. It's the only way we can get them to stop."

"We can't battle them all," said Wayne. "We have to keep fighting them while we search for the spawner. I know it sounds impossible, but it's the only way."

"Do you have any idea where the spawner might be?" asked Billy as he slammed his sword into the belly of a skeleton.

"I think it has to be between Farmer's Bay and Verdant Valley," replied Wayne.

As the gang battled the skeletons, Edison heard a familiar voice call out to them, and he turned around.

"Edison!" Anna cried. "Oh no! Your town is being invaded too!"

"Wow." Wayne was surprised. "Two towns are under attack. I've never seen that before. This is going to be harder than I originally thought."

"We have to find the spawner," said Billy.

Anna ran through the town, clutching a bottle of potion with one hand and a sword in the other. She splashed skeletons and slew them as she raced toward Edison.

"How can we stop this?" asked Anna.

"We have to find the spawner. There must be one close by," explained Wayne.

"Let's go find it now," ordered Edison.

4
SEARCH FOR THE SPAWNER

"How can we leave now?" Peyton shouted as new skeletons spawned around them. "We can't abandon our town!"

"It's the only way we can really help them." Wayne raced through the dark night, carefully dodging arrows being shot in all directions.

Edison and the others followed closely behind. "Where are we going?" Edison called out as they reached Verdant Valley.

Skeletons emerging from Verdant Valley and Farmer's Bay chased the group, and they were stuck in another battle with the bony beasts.

"Why did you lead us here?" Billy hollered at Wayne. "This is the worst spot. We have to battle skeletons from both towns. This is a death trap."

Wayne breathlessly replied, "I thought there would be a cave between here and Verdant Valley. This is what the criminal behind these attacks usually does: He places the spawner between towns so that people have to battle hordes of skeletons that spawn in both locations. He wants to weaken people and destroy communities. I told you he was tricky." He slammed his sword into two skeletons.

"I'm out of potions," Edison cried. Since he was an expert alchemist, he relied on his potions in battle and not his skill as a good swordsman. His hearts were low as he ripped into a skeleton while a sea of arrows struck his exposed arms, and he respawned in his bed.

Puddles meowed by the side of his bed. Edison didn't want to get up and battle the skeletons. He looked at his brewing stand in the corner of the room and felt it calling to him. If only he could spend the day working on the potion of invisibility, he would have a chance at winning the brewing competition. As he sat up, he looked through his inventory. It was incredibly low. He only had a few apples for food, and there weren't any potions left to help in battle. He told himself there was no point in teleporting back to his friends to help them when he didn't have the necessary supplies to survive. Using this logic, Edison planned on getting to work on a batch of potions. He had a bunch of new bottles he could use and was about to step over to the brewing stand when he saw sunlight through his bedroom window. He quickly raced to the window and looked out at the peaceful, quiet road. Edison left his home, making a mental note that he had to repair his door.

"Billy!" He opened Billy's door and walked through

Billy's bungalow looking for his friend, but he wasn't there.

Edison left and went to Peyton's house, but she wasn't there, and neither was Erin. He raced to the shore and was relieved to find Erin's pirate ship still docked. He climbed the mammoth ladder to the top of the ship and called out for his friends, but the ship was empty.

This is so strange, Edison thought as he climbed down the ladder. He headed out of Farmer's Bay and toward Verdant Valley. His first stop was Anna's house, but he was upset to discover that it was also empty. When he reached the castle, as he hurried over the moat, Edison could hear the murmur of people talking and was hopeful he'd find his friends.

"Edison," Anna called out, "we're over here."

Edison spotted Anna in the lavish gardens. She was talking to Dante and Gregson. Racing toward them, he looked for the others, but they were nowhere in sight.

"Where is everybody?" asked Edison.

"They're inside," Anna replied. "We were able to locate the skeleton spawner last night, and they're eating now. Everybody's tired."

Edison felt bad, as if he hadn't helped his friends enough. He wished he had been there to deactivate the spawner, and he promised himself he wouldn't let them down again.

"I feel awful about not helping you guys last night," confessed Edison.

"Why?" questioned Anna. "You did help us. It's not

your fault you were destroyed by skeletons. We found the spawner right after that. There was nothing you could have done."

Anna's explanation made Edison feel a bit better, but he was left with many questions. "Where did you find the spawner?"

"It was in the old mineshaft next to the castle," said Anna.

"Did you see the person Wayne said was behind all of these skeleton attacks? Were you able to capture him?"

"No," Anna said, "but we will. We've solved mysteries before, and we're going to find out who is directing these attacks."

"I want to go inside and talk to Wayne." Edison excused himself and joined the others inside the castle.

Peyton was chewing when she saw Edison walk into the castle, so she put her hand over her mouth as she invited Edison to join them for an impromptu celebratory breakfast feast. "Dante gave us all of this food because he was so glad we deactivated the spawner."

"I'm sorry I couldn't help you guys," Edison told the group. He picked a freshly baked cookie from a tray and took a bite.

Billy was in detective mode. "I've been talking to Wayne, and he has an idea where this person will strike next."

Edison swallowed his cookie and asked, "Really? How?"

Wayne said, "I just came up with an idea. It might

be crazy, but I've noticed a pattern. He seems to focus on various biomes. The first attack was in the jungle, then the desert, and now the shoreline. I bet the next attack will be in the Cold Taiga Biome."

Edison didn't think this pattern made sense. He also wanted to know why Wayne believed the attack was over. The person who was attacking them didn't win anything. He questioned, "Why do you believe Farmer's Bay and Verdant Valley are safe from attacks? Whoever is behind them didn't get anything from us at all. Wouldn't they attack again until we were so weak, we'd give over everything we have? Just like you had said they would?"

"That's a good point. But we can leave a few people here to battle the skeletons if they spawn again, and we could head to the Cold Taiga Biome to catch them before they begin the next attack."

"That's a great idea," said Billy. "You, me, and Edison can go to the biome and see if this person is setting up the next attack."

Edison only had six days before the brewing competition, and a trip to the Cold Taiga Biome would throw him off schedule. He was already having trouble brewing the potion of invisibility, which was one of the potions he was usually quite skilled at crafting. He had to keep practicing in order to have a chance at winning any medals at the competition.

"Usually, I'd love to help, but I have to stick around here. I'm in a brewing competition that is taking place in Verdant Valley in less than a week, and I don't think I should leave."

As Edison spoke, Dante escorted into the castle a group of people wearing T-shirts that read ALCHEMIST OLYMPICS in big black bold letters.

"The crew is here for the brewing competition," announced Dante.

Omar walked over to the group. "Hi, I'm Omar," he introduced himself. "Dante asked me to help you build the stage for the competition."

"Thanks, Omar. We were looking for you," a woman with pink hair said. "Great to meet you all. I'm Luna. I'm the head of the brewing competition. We can't wait to have the competition here in Verdant Valley, it's such a great town."

Wayne said, "I'm afraid this might not be the place to hold a brewing competition."

"What?" Luna was shocked.

"This town and the neighboring one, Farmer's Bay, are under attack," Wayne explained.

"I don't see anybody attacking Verdant Valley." Luna looked around.

"Yesterday someone placed a skeleton spawner in an abandoned mineshaft and staged a skeleton attack of epic proportions."

"Wow," Luna gasped. "I wasn't aware of this." She looked at everyone. "Are you guys okay?"

They nodded their heads. Peyton spoke. "It was a terrifying and exhausting attack, but hopefully it's over."

"It's not over," declared Wayne. "You'll see. This is just the beginning."

Edison was annoyed and wanted Wayne to stop talking and leave the town. He felt that ever since Wayne arrived, there had been trouble. He looked at Wayne and realized he had his first suspect.

5

BUSINESS AS USUAL

"We've been planning this competition for months. In less than a week, we will have the greatest alchemists from around the Overworld arriving to stay here," explained Luna. "This town better not be under attack."

"It should be fine," Dante reassured Luna. "The spawner was deactivated last night. You can start setting up for the competition."

"Great," Luna said as she walked out of the castle with Dante, Omar, and the group of people from the competition.

Wayne was visibly upset. He paced around the dining table and yelled at everyone, "You guys are crazy. You shouldn't have let them go and plan a competition. This is serious."

"Why don't we be the judges of how serious the

attack is? Maybe since we deactivated the spawner, the attack is over," stated Edison.

"You weren't even there when we deactivated the spawner. You care about the alchemy competition just because you're probably in it," said Wayne.

"It doesn't matter if I'm in the competition," Edison defended himself.

"So you are?" asked Wayne.

Anna didn't want to see them fight, so she interrupted, "I have a great idea. Why don't we go to the Cold Taiga Biome and search for the person behind these attacks and let Edison stay here? He's a great alchemist, and he deserves to be in this competition. It's a once-in-a-lifetime opportunity for him, don't you understand?"

Wayne said, "My town was so destroyed by this person and these skeleton attacks—I'm only trying to help you."

Edison was torn. He wanted to help, but he also wanted to participate in the competition.

Edison felt much better when Billy said, "I'll go with Anna and Wayne. You worked much too hard to get sidetracked by this. Stay here and be in the competition. I will try my hardest to return in time to watch you win a medal."

"I don't know if I'll win a medal, but I hope you can make it," said Edison, and then he watched Billy and Anna leave the castle with Wayne.

"See?" Amira said to Edison. "Everything is going to be all right."

Edison hoped Amira was correct, but he couldn't help feeling worried about Billy and Anna. There was something that he didn't trust about Wayne, and he hoped they'd be okay.

Back at the brewing station, Edison wasn't getting anything right. His mind was on his friends. He wanted to see how they were doing, but he knew he had to pay attention and practice for the competition.

I can't let them down, he told himself as he stared at the bottles and the ingredients. He was frozen. He didn't know what to make, and he wished Billy were there beside him. After a minute or so, he decided to craft another potion of invisibility. He placed another fermented spider eye into a potion of night vision, and this time he clutched the stopwatch and pressed the button when he took his first sip. He stared at the stopwatch, but when the potion wore off, the stopwatch wasn't in his hand. He looked down and saw it lying on the floor.

What happened? Edison said to himself as he rubbed his eyes. He was shocked when he heard someone respond.

"Edison." Amira stood at the door. "Are you okay?"

"I don't know," he replied.

Amira pointed to the broken door. "I came by because it's almost nighttime and I was worried that you hadn't fixed your door."

"Almost nighttime?" Edison was confused. It was the afternoon when he sipped the potion, and he wondered how long he was invisible. He picked up the stopwatch, but it was off. It must have turned off when he dropped it.

Amira picked up the door. "You seem really tired. Let me fix this for you."

"I can help." Edison walked to the door, but he felt dizzy and stopped.

"Are you okay?"

"There must be something wrong with the batch of the potion of invisibility I made. Every time I take it, it seems to grow stronger and really bothers me. I'm thinking that I might have to drop out of the competition."

"Drop out? No way. You're one of the best alchemists I know. Is there anything I can do to help?" Amira asked as she placed the door in the entranceway.

Edison helped her repair the door. "I don't know. Billy was helping me. Maybe you can time me and see how long I am invisible and if I disappear."

"Disappear?" Amira questioned as they finished the repair. She closed the door behind her and walked over to Edison's brewing table.

"Yes, it seems as if the potion of invisibility is so strong that it makes me disappear."

"I've never heard of that before," said Amira.

"I know, it's very strange. I have to figure out what is happening and why it's so strong," said Edison.

"Why don't you brew a new batch now, and I'll time you. And I'll see if you disappear," Amira suggested and picked up the stopwatch.

Edison carefully brewed a single potion of invisibility and slowly took a small sip.

Amira pressed the stopwatch when he wasn't visible, "Are you still there?" she asked.

"Yes," he replied.

After a minute went by, she asked again. "Are you still there?"

"Yes," Edison replied.

The third time she asked him, Amira noticed his voice grow fainter. She was about to call to him again but was jarred when she heard the sound of rattling bones outside of the house. She held the stopwatch and ran to the window. A skeleton army was off in the distance. Amira placed the stopwatch on the brewing station and pulled armor from her inventory. "Oh no, Edison! When is this going to wear off?"

There was no reply. She picked up the stopwatch as the sounds of the rattling bones grew louder, and she readied herself for an attack. She held a diamond sword in one hand and the stopwatch in the other.

"Edison!" Amira shouted. "It looks like there's another skeleton invasion!"

She looked at the stopwatch and was in shock when it went over thirty minutes. She had taken the potion of invisibility many times, and it had never lasted this long.

"Edison!"

She could hear the sound of clanging bones outside the door. The army was approaching. She called out to Edison again, but there was no reply.

6
I CAN'T SEE YOU

"**E**dison!" Amira screamed.

She didn't wait for the skeletons to break down the door as she rushed out into the thick of the battle.

Peyton obliterated two skeletons as she shouted, "Wayne warned us about this. He told us that we'd have another invasion."

Erin annihilated a skeleton when she spotted Amira coming out of Edison's house. "Where's Edison? Is he still in there brewing potions? Too busy to come out here and help us?"

"He disappeared." Amira's voice cracked as she plunged her diamond sword into a bony skeleton leg.

"What? He abandoned us?" Peyton was infuriated, and she took it out on the skeletons that shot a barrage of arrows in her direction. Despite the pain radiating down her left arm after being struck by two arrows and the fact that she had only one heart left, Peyton used her last bit of strength to lunge at the skeletons and slam her swords into them, destroying them both. She quickly grabbed a potion from her inventory to regain her energy, but the bottle was empty.

"I need more potions." She raced toward Edison's house. "I need to talk to Edison."

Amira battled three skeletons, yet she could still see Peyton bolting through the open door of Edison's bungalow. "He's not in there. I told you he's missing."

"I see him," Peyton called out from the entranceway.

Amira was desperate to find out where Edison had been, but the skeletons were putting up a tough fight, and she was losing hearts. She struck the skeletons, yet they weren't getting any weaker.

"Help!" Amira yelled as the skeletons cornered her.

Erin rushed over and struck one skeleton, destroying it. "They're weak, just strike them."

With one eye on the entrance to Edison's house, she ripped into the skeletons, finally annihilated the beasts, and placed their dropped bones in her inventory.

Puddles meowed by the entrance to the house. Edison stood by his brewing station as Peyton lectured him. "You didn't want to travel to the Cold Taiga Biome with Wayne, Anna, and Billy, and now you're not helping the town as we deal with this serious skeleton invasion."

Edison just stood silently, grasping the edge of the brewing station, trying not to fall down. Peyton continued, "What is wrong with you? Don't you care about

Farmer's Bay? Or do you only care about the brewing competition? I bet if this continues, they'll cancel it and then you'll never get an award."

Edison said nothing, which made Peyton even angrier. "Why aren't you saying anything?"

Edison finally replied. His face was white as a sheet, and his voice was faint as he said, "I need milk."

"Milk?" Peyton was confused.

Amira rushed toward her friend Edison while pulling a cup of milk from her inventory and handing it to him. "Here, drink this slowly. Are you okay?"

Edison took a sip of the milk. "I disappeared again. Didn't I?"

"Yes," said Amira.

"What's he talking about?" asked Peyton. Noticing Edison's weakened state, she felt bad that she had yelled at him. "Is he sick?"

The milk brought color back to Edison's pale face. "It seems that every time I brew a batch of the potion of invisibility, it's so strong that it makes me disappear."

"Where do you go?" asked Peyton.

"I'm not sure I go anywhere. I think it might put me to sleep or something. I don't remember. When the potion wears off, it leaves me very tired."

"When did this start?" asked Amira. "You seemed fine yesterday, when we dropped off all of the bottles."

Edison thought for a moment. He realized this all began when Amira and Omar returned to town. "Right after you arrived. When you came over and left these bottles, afterward I took the potion I had brewed, and when I awoke, Billy was in the middle of battling skeletons."

Amira wondered if her arrival could have anything to do with this sudden invasion. Could there have been a stowaway on their ship? Did they come to shore and cause all of this trouble? "That's strange. I wonder if it does have anything to do with us. Maybe someone was hiding in the ship. Dante's ship is so large it's a possibility," said Amira.

"I bet she's right," said Peyton. "Someone was probably hiding out on your ship."

Edison had another idea. "Didn't you come back to see me in the brewing competition?"

Amira nodded her head.

Edison said, "I think that's the reason this is all happening. I believe someone doesn't want the competition to happen."

"That doesn't account for the potion of invisibility that makes you disappear," added Amira.

"No, but I bet if we figure out who is behind all of these skeleton attacks, we'll discover something about this unusually strong potion," said Edison.

Bones clanged outside the window, and Edison saw a skeleton aiming its arrow through the glass. "We have to find the spawner."

"Do you think it's back in the same mineshaft?" asked Peyton.

"I don't know, but we're going to have to look," said Edison.

The trio galloped through the dark night. As they

reached the outskirts of Verdant Valley, two creepers silently lurked behind Peyton. *Kaboom!* Peyton didn't have the chance to turn around—she was destroyed.

"Should we go back and get Peyton?" asked Amira.

"I think we have to find the spawner, and we have to do it fast." Edison pointed to the seemingly never-ending group of skeletons marching out of Verdant Valley and straight toward the duo. The skeletons aimed their arrows and were about to shoot.

"How are we going to get past the skeleton army?" Amira held her sword, ready to battle the group, but she knew it was pointless. There were too many to fight.

"We're not," said Edison and he rushed toward a small hill next to them. "Follow me!"

"Where?"

"Can you see this?" He turned around, relieved to find Amira behind him. He ducked his head into the cave's opening, "I used to go mining here ages ago. I almost forgot it existed until I needed gold to make a golden carrot for the potion of night vision, and I mined here and found gold."

"You found gold here?" Amira lit a torch. "In this small cave?"

Click! Clang! The sounds of skeletons shook the dirt walls of the cave.

"I think we found the spawner," said Edison.

7

TREASURES OR TROUBLE?

There was a large hole in the ground. Edison pointed down to the blocky crater. "And this is where I found tons of gold, which I didn't expect. I was shocked."

The vibrations from the skeleton army shook the small musty cave. Amira held her torch, trying to use the little light they had to find the spawner. The rattling was almost deafening.

"It sounds like this skeleton army is massive," said Edison.

"We're not going to withstand an attack of this magnitude." Amira searched her inventory, but it was almost empty. She didn't have enough supplies to beat the army.

Edison pulled out a potion of swiftness. "I hope this isn't as strong as the potion of invisibility."

They gulped the potion, racing past the army with

only a few arrows piercing through their exposed arms. The pain was overwhelming, but they knew it was a small sacrifice for deactivating the spawner.

"I see it!" Amira screamed. She held her torch in one hand and a sword in the other as she raced toward the spawner. Amira placed her torch atop the spawner and pulled out another torch to put on the side. "Oh no! I'm out of torches. We need more torches."

Edison looked through his inventory and sighed with relief when he found four torches. He quickly pulled them out and placed them around the spawner, instantly deactivating it.

"Now we've stopped them from spawning, but we still have to battle the existing skeletons."

The duo sprinted from the cave, ready for battle, but sunlight shone through the cave's entrance.

"It's daylight!" Amira exclaimed.

"We have to tell the others that there was another spawner." Edison walked in the direction of Farmer's Bay, but a voice called out to him. He turned around to see Luna.

"Edison," Luna informed him, "we had a severe skeleton attack yesterday, and many members of the committee are worried that we can't hold the competition here."

"What? Really?" Edison's heart raced. He had been preparing for this competition for such a long time, and these words were devastating to him. They couldn't cancel the competition.

"We don't feel we can invite people to this

competition and jeopardize their safety. It isn't right," said Luna.

"We have to stop the attacks," said Edison.

"Of course," Luna sighed, "but how?"

Edison thought about Billy. He was off with Wayne in the Cold Taiga Biome searching for the person who was behind these attacks. He thought of joining them, but he also had another plan. A plan that might possibly save the competition and wouldn't require him to travel far.

"We need to get a team together to battle the attacker. We must secure every mineshaft or other location where they might put a skeleton spawner. Once we do that we won't have another attack," suggested Edison.

"Good idea," Luna said and then clarified, "but it's just an idea. If you stop any further skeleton invasions while also finding out who is behind these attacks, we will continue with the competition. But for now, it's canceled."

"Canceled!" Edison's voice cracked as he pleaded, "Don't cancel it."

"We have to. I'm sorry. I told you we will hold it if you are able to do those two things," said Luna.

Edison wanted her to know that those were two impossible requests, but he desperately wanted the competition to take place, so he said, "I promise you I will find out who is behind these attacks and I will make sure they're stopped."

"I hope you keep your promise," said Luna. "I guess

we'll find out soon." Luna walked back to Verdant Valley.

As he watched her walk off in the distance, Edison thought about the promise he had just made. He knew he had made a promise he might not be able to keep, but he would work his hardest to make sure he found out who was behind these attacks. Since his first and only suspect was traveling with Billy and Anna in the cold biome, Edison knew he had to go there. However, first he needed to make sure this town was secure. He was going back to Farmer's Bay to call a town meeting.

"You promised Luna a lot," said Anna.

"I know. Will you help me?"

"Of course," Amira said and then asked if she could have one last look at the cave. "Do you have a torch?"

Edison picked his last torch from his inventory and handed it to Amira. "Why do you want to go back to the cave?"

She didn't respond. Instead she carefully inspected the blocky patch where Edison had said he found gold. "You said this is the place where you found the gold, right?"

"Yes."

Amira picked up her pickaxe and banged against a block. She quickly removed a few layers, but she didn't find any gold. "There's nothing here."

"I mined it all."

"No," Amira said. "Before I began my life at sea, I was a pretty good miner. I know where you find one mineral, you often find another. Maybe it's not as good as diamonds or gold, but this seems to be a mine that was used so many times it has nothing left."

"What are you saying?" asked Edison.

"I think someone placed that gold here. They wanted you or another alchemist to find it," said Amira.

"I bet it's the same person who placed the spawner," added Edison.

"I agree." Amira put away her pickaxe and walked toward the exit.

"But who?" asked Edison. Although he usually played the role of detective, he realized that he was too attached to the brewing competition, and he might not be levelheaded enough to solve this crime.

"I don't know, but I'm going to help you find out," said Amira.

Edison was grateful for the help. He knew Amira would keep him on track, and he had made a huge and potentially impossible promise to the head of the brewing competition. Now he needed all the help he could get.

As the duo exited the cave, they heard the sound of a pickaxe banging against the blocky dirt.

"What was that?" Amira paused by the cave's entrance.

"I don't know, but we're going to find out." Edison held his sword tightly and headed deeper into the dark musty cave.

8
GOLD

Edison and Amira crept deeper into the dark cave as they shared Edison's last torch. They tried to creep soundlessly toward the chopping noise. They reached the end of the cave, and Edison gasped when he came in full view of someone in a black jacket banging a pickaxe against the wall of the cave.

"Wayne," Edison called out, "what are you doing here?"

The stranger turned around, but although the miner was dressed in a black jacket and had messy red hair like Wayne, it wasn't Wayne. The mysterious person didn't speak, but splashed a potion of invisibility on the ground and disappeared.

Edison spotted the pickaxe still floating in the air and tried to swing his enchanted diamond sword at the invisible person, but it was too late. The pickaxe went away, and Edison knew the battle was over.

"What was that?" asked Edison.

"Who was that?" questioned Amira.

"I think we have to go to the Cold Taiga Biome. I think Wayne knows a lot more than he is telling us. That guy was dressed just like him."

Amira agreed. "Yes, he wore the same black jacket. It seems like they're a part of an army or something."

"We should teleport to Billy and Anna," suggested Edison.

As the duo got ready to teleport, they were unaware of the crop of creepers that silently crept behind them, and within seconds they were both in their own beds. Edison spawned in the bungalow and Amira on the ship.

Edison rubbed his eyes as he got out of bed and walked over to a chest in the corner of his room, searching for items that would be useful in the Cold Taiga Biome. He had only been to that biome once before. He had traveled there with Billy, and it had turned out to be one of their favorite days. They had built a snowman and had a snowball fight. They were there on a treasure hunt, but they never found any treasures, and it didn't matter. Now Edison was returning to the biome to find his friend. He hoped he was okay, even though he wasn't sure if Wayne was on their side. Maybe he was a rogue soldier or the trickster who was behind the attacks, and Edison needed to find out.

Puddles meowed as Edison searched through the chest, and he pulled fish from his inventory to feed the ocelot. As Puddles ate, Edison filled his inventory with another sword and a few more torches, and then he looked at his brewing station. He needed to brew more potions for the trip. He wasn't going to be able to save his friends if he didn't have any potions.

Edison stood at the brewing stand crafting a potion of instant health. He placed Nether wart and a glistering melon into one of the new bottles that Amira and Omar had given him. Suddenly Amira walked in.

"I thought we were supposed to be saving our friends, not brewing potions." Amira was annoyed. "Didn't you hear the competition isn't going to happen if we don't stop these attacks?"

"I'm sorry," said Edison. "I don't have any potions left in my inventory, and I felt that we need to have the proper supplies in order to help our friends."

"I guess you're right," said Amira. "We just have to do this quickly. It's getting late, and I don't want to teleport there in the middle of the night."

Edison worked as quickly as he could because he knew Amira was right and they had to leave soon. While he brewed batches of various potions, Amira inspected the gold bars and a carrot he had left on the table.

"Is this the golden carrot you used to brew the potion of invisibility that makes you disappear?" She held the gold bar.

"Yes." He looked up as he put more blaze powder down to refuel his brewing stand.

"I know we're pressed for time, but can you brew a potion of night vision and invisibility with one of my gold bars?" Amira pulled a bar from her inventory and handed it to Edison.

"Sure. Why?"

"I want to see if it's as strong as before. I think something is wrong with the bars you found in that cave. I think someone left them there to hurt you or another alchemist during the competition. They wanted them to lose the potion of invisibility brewing contest."

Edison used the gold bar and brewed a potion of night vision, adding the fermented spider eye to the potion. He took a sip. Amira watched Edison disappear.

"Edison," Amira said, "talk to me."

"I'm here," he replied.

"I have an idea. Take out your diamond sword and hold it so I know you're still here."

Edison grasped the sword, and within minutes he reappeared. He wasn't groggy, and although Amira didn't time how long he was gone, he knew it was the way a normal potion of invisibility worked.

Amira held on to the gold blocks. "Do you have any more of these?"

Edison walked over to a chest and opened it. The gold glistened as he lifted the top of the chest. "This is the batch."

"You found all that in the cave?"

"Yes," said Edison. "It was an amazing mining trip."

"Too amazing." Amira placed the blocks in the chest. "I want to put all of the blocks in the same chest so we know where they are. You shouldn't use them again. In fact, we should bring them to Luna and show her that someone is tampering with the ingredients."

Amira picked up the chest and put it in her inventory. "Let's see Luna, and then we'll go to the icy biome."

The duo jogged to Verdant Valley. Omar was building the stage for the competition. He called out a greeting to Edison and Amira.

Edison said, "I'm glad you're still building the stage, Omar. I'm hoping they don't cancel the competition."

"Me too," said Omar.

Amira asked, "Have you seen Luna? We have something to show her."

Omar pointed to the castle. "She's in there. We're still planning as if the competition is going to go on. She is probably in a meeting. Luna is very busy."

As Edison and Amira hurried toward the castle, Edison looked back at the stage. He hoped he'd be able to brew a proper potion of invisibility on the stage and that he and his fellow participants would have a fair chance of winning the competition.

9
IN THE CASTLE

Luna was very busy, and she told Edison and Amira, "I'm sorry, I don't have time to speak to you guys now. We're behind schedule—*if* the competition even takes place."

"We have something important to show you," Amira said, "that has to do with the contest."

"Did you secure Verdant Valley?"

Amira and Edison fumbled with a response.

"If you didn't, we don't have anything to speak about, and you should leave," she said as she walked them to the door.

Amira pulled the chest from her inventory and opened it. "These are tainted gold bars."

"What are you talking about?" asked Luna. She moved away from Amira and walked over to a group of people wearing T-shirts with ALCHEMIST OLYMPICS in big black bold letters.

Amira stepped into the middle of the group. "Edison went mining in a small cave right outside of Verdant Valley and found all of these gold bars. He brewed a bunch of batches of the potion of invisibility with them, and then he disappeared."

Luna looked confused. "Isn't that what's supposed to happen when you consume the potion of invisibility?" All of the people around her shook their heads as she asked Amira and Edison this question.

Edison pulled out the last two batches of the potion he had brewed with the bars. "Do you want to try this?"

"I told you, I don't have any time for this," Luna protested.

"Please, you'll see that someone is trying to sabotage the contest," pleaded Edison.

"I know they are trying to destroy it. There have been intense skeleton attacks." Luna tried to walk away, but Edison followed after her and gulped the potion.

Edison became invisible, but he grabbed his sword and said, "I want you to watch this sword." His voice grew fainter as he spoke.

Within a minute, the sword was gone. Luna asked, "Is this some sort of trick? Did he teleport somewhere?"

"It's not a trick. Someone left these gold bars in a cave near Verdant Valley because they wanted one of the alchemists to use them and lose the competition," explained Amira.

"Where's Edison?" Luna called out.

The people from the Alchemist Olympics talked over each other, yet they all said the same thing. They had never seen anyone stay invisible this long or disappear.

"When is Edison coming back? When is this trick over? If he doesn't become visible soon, I will disqualify him from the competition," declared Luna.

"You can't do that," Amira begged. "He didn't do anything wrong. He was just trying to prove a serious point. This contest is under attack, and someone is trying to ruin it."

"Let me look at this gold." Luna picked up a piece of gold from the chest. "It looks just like every other piece of gold I've seen before. How do you know there's something wrong with it?"

Amira replied, "Brew something with it."

"I don't have time to do that," said Luna.

"Have someone working here do it. They'll see that there's a problem with the gold," explained Amira.

Edison reappeared as Dante walked in. "Edison, are you okay?" Dante rushed over to him.

Edison held on to Dante's shoulder and spoke softly. "I need to eat."

"Yes." Dante grabbed an apple and handed it to him.

The color came back to his pale face as he chewed the apple.

"Is this some sort of trick? A magic show?" Luna was annoyed.

"No," Amira replied. "Test this gold, and you'll get all the answers you'll need. We have to go to the Cold Taiga Biome and see if we can help our friends."

Dante asked, "Edison, are you strong enough to teleport to there?"

Edison finished the apple, but he was still low on hearts. He picked up the potion of instant health from his inventory and gulped it down. "Yes, I'll be okay. I have to find out who is behind all of this. I made a promise to Luna that I will do everything I can to make sure the Alchemist Olympics are going to happen in Verdant Valley, and I'm going to keep the promise."

Amira and Edison were ready to teleport when Wayne walked into the room.

"Don't bother going to the Cold Taiga Biome to find your friends," Wayne announced.

"Wayne!" Amira rushed over to him. "What are you talking about? Are they okay?"

"They're missing," he said, and Edison thought he saw Wayne smirk.

10

POLAR BEARS

"Tell us what happened to our friends." Edison pulled out his sword, aiming it at Wayne.

"What are you doing?" Luna cried out. "Don't attack him."

"Please put your sword down. I'm not the enemy," Wayne pleaded. "If you put down the sword, I'll tell you what happened."

"Okay." Edison placed the sword back in his inventory. "What happened to my friends? And tell us quickly, because if they're in any kind of trouble, I want to save them now."

"I have a confession," Wayne announced. "Before I tell you about your friends, I must let you know that I was originally behind this attack. I was trying to ruin the competition. I had a partner, Brett, but we had a fight, and to get back at him, I decided to destroy our original plan. When he saw me run toward the town and alert you guys that there was a skeleton spawner, he was furious. I knew he was going to the Cold Taiga Biome next, and I needed help fighting him, which is why I enlisted your friends."

"What does this person look like?" asked Amira.

"He wears a black jacket like mine," he said as he pointed to his jacket, "and we have the same hair color."

Amira and Edison believed he was telling the truth because they had encountered a person in a black jacket in the cave.

"You haven't told us what happened to our friends!" demanded Edison.

"I don't know. I was with them in the Cold Taiga Biome when I spotted a polar bear. I tried not to provoke it, but it became very aggressive. I called for help, but nobody came. I tried to fight the bear with my diamond sword, but I was weak, and it destroyed me. When I respawned in the igloo, your friends were missing. I've been looking for them, and I can't find them. I'm really worried." Wayne sounded sincere.

Edison hoped he wasn't falling for a trick, but he had no choice but to travel to the cold biome and look for his friends. "We're going to the cold biome with you. We need to find our friends."

Luna worried that the skeleton attacks would continue and expressed her concern. "Before you guys leave, are you sure all of the skeleton spawners are deactivated? I don't think we can survive another attack tonight and still have the competition continue."

"I deactivated the one in the cave." Edison looked

at Wayne. "Are there any other spawners that we should deactivate?"

"No," Wayne said. "There aren't any more, or at least I don't know of any others. Maybe Brett put one somewhere, but I doubt it."

"We saw him trying to dig a tunnel in the cave outside of Verdant Valley," said Amira.

"You saw him?" Wayne was shocked.

"Yes, when we were deactivating the spawner," said Edison.

Wayne informed Luna and the others, "You should keep an eye on that cave. That was where Brett and I had originally set everything up. He will most likely return there."

Amira looked out the window. "We have to get to the Cold Taiga Biome before nightfall."

Wayne pulled a map out of his inventory. "It's not too far away." He pointed to the mountainous biome that they needed to go through to reach their destination.

Edison looked at the map. He had only traveled over the mountains once, on the treasure hunt with Billy, but this time it wasn't for a fun treasure hunt. He had to find his friends.

The trio climbed the steep mountains, not paying attention to the stunning views but focusing on getting to the Cold Taiga Biome before dark. When they reached the bottom of the mountain, they were exhausted. Edison pulled milk from his inventory and offered it to Amira and Wayne.

They took a sip as Wayne pointed at an igloo in the distance. "That's where we were staying."

Amira looked up at the sky. "It's getting dark. We should hurry to the igloo."

Snow covered most of the biome, and the ground was slick and icy. The gang raced to the igloo as they tried not to slip on the ice, but Edison stopped when he saw something dash by and run behind a snow-covered spruce tree. Edison's feet were wet, and he tried to avoid stepping in the snow. There were still patches of grass, so Edison stood on a grassy spot trying to fig-ure out what had run past them.

"Edison," Amira asked, "why did you stop?"

"Did you see anything run by us?" While he spoke the figure dashed by again.

"I think that's just a wolf," said Wayne. "We can't stop. We have to make it to the igloo."

They were inches from the igloo when two polar bears lumbered by them. They ran toward the igloo, but the polar bears mistook their rushing to the igloo as an attack. One of the large white bears stood on its hind legs and unleashed a loud roar.

Edison stared at the bear's mouth filled with enor-mous sharp teeth. As he headed for the igloo's entrance, he tried to slip past the bears without a battle, but it was too late. Both bears leaped at Edison, Wayne, and Amira.

Amira's diamond sword sliced into the white mat-ted fur of one of the bears as Wayne pierced the belly of the other bear. Edison stood next to Amira as he slammed his sword into the bear until it was destroyed, and Wayne singlehandedly annihilated the other bear.

"Last time I was the one who lost the battle with the bear," Wayne confessed.

Both bears dropped raw salmon on the snowy ground.

Amira picked up the salmon and handed it to Edison. "Take it for Puddles."

"This is a rare treat." Edison stared at the salmon in Amira's hand. "I don't think we should give it to Puddles. Why don't we have a big dinner tomorrow after we find everyone and celebrate?"

Amira placed the salmon in her inventory. "That sounds like a great plan."

The trio entered the igloo, and Edison glanced at his friends' empty beds. He hoped he'd be able to find them. He wanted a reason to eat the salmon and to celebrate their return. He couldn't believe that just a few days before, all he could think about was winning the brewing competition, and now he was responsible for stopping these attacks and enabling the competition to continue.

Edison crawled into a bed and asked Wayne, "Who slept in this bed?"

"That's Billy's bed," replied Wayne as he looked up from under the covers of the other bed.

Edison's heart sunk. He missed his friend, and he hoped he could find him.

11

ICY MESS

The sun glistened through the small window of the igloo, melting a layer of blocky ice. Edison jumped out of bed. He was eager to find his friends and stop Brett, who was supposedly behind this attack. When he got out of bed, he looked over at the empty beds and realized he was the only one in the igloo. He raced out the small door and into a polar bear.

Roaarrr!

The polar bear let out a powerful growl as it swiped its large paw at Edison. Edison stared into the bear's black eyes while he grabbed a sword from his inventory. The bear's paw ripped through his arm, scratching into his flesh. Edison wailed as he painfully drew his sword and struck the bear until it dropped salmon on the ground.

"Edison!" Amira called out.

Edison turned around and spotted Amira racing toward him. He asked, "Where's Wayne?"

"I have to tell you something about Wayne." Amira trembled as she spoke. "I woke up very early and I saw him get out of bed and leave the igloo. I decided to follow him. I quietly trailed behind him, and I saw Wayne meet the person in the black jacket that we saw in the cave. I don't think we should trust him."

"Did he see you?"

Amira took a deep breath, exhaled, and said, "I hope he didn't see me. I don't think so. They were in the middle of an intense conversation."

"Where were they?"

Amira pointed in the direction of a snow-capped mountain. "In a cave in that mountain."

"Did you see Billy and Anna?" asked Edison. This new information about Wayne made him very concerned for his friends' safety.

"No," Amira said, "but we have to find them."

"Can you show me where you saw Wayne?" asked Edison.

Before Amira could respond, Wayne walked over to them. "Great, you guys are up and ready to help."

Amira and Edison stared at each other. They didn't have time to come up with a plan on how they should deal with Wayne. Amira was the first to speak, questioning Wayne. "Where were you? We woke up and you were gone."

Wayne told them a story about wolves. "I heard scratching outside and howling. I went to investigate and saw a pack of wolves. I tried to tame them, but it didn't work. The pack surrounded me and tried to bite me. I had to destroy them. Once that battle was done, I heard a noise in the distance and went to see what it might be, but it was nothing."

Amira couldn't believe Wayne was standing in front of them telling a made-up story. She didn't have the patience or interest in playing along and said, "I saw you. I know where you were."

"What?" Wayne was surprised. "I have no idea what you're talking about. If you saw me, you would have seen me battling the wolves."

"I saw you talking to Brett. Tell us what is going on, Wayne." Amira pulled out her enchanted diamond sword and held it close to Wayne's chest.

"Why were you talking to Brett?" asked Amira.

Wayne pulled a potion from his inventory, but before he could splash it on himself Edison warned him, "You better not make yourself disappear, because we'll find you. Tell us what's going on."

"Are you working with Brett?" asked Amira.

"No," Wayne replied.

"Then why were you talking to him?" questioned Edison.

"It's not what you think," said Wayne.

"What I think is that our friends are missing and you have something to do with it," said Amira.

Wayne tried to flee from them, but he slipped on the icy ground and steadied himself by holding on to the bark of a spruce tree.

Edison aimed his sword at Wayne. "Tell us where our friends are. We want to know."

Wayne stuttered as he put the bottle of potion away and replied, "I don't know where your friends are, but Brett does."

"Take us to Brett," ordered Amira as she pointed her sword toward his unarmored chest.

"Stop!" Wayne cried. "I'll show you where he is."

Wayne headed in the direction of the icy cave where Amira had spotted he and Brett earlier that morning. Amira and Edison followed closely behind carrying their swords, letting Wayne know that if he led them in the wrong direction, they weren't afraid to strike him.

"Brett?" Wayne peeked his head into the icy cave.

Brett responded, "Why are you here?"

Edison whispered to Wayne, "Don't tell him we're with you. We want to surprise him."

"Brett, please come here." Wayne's voice cracked.

Brett hurried into the front of the cave, but he wasn't surprised when he saw Amira and Edison standing next to Wayne. Instead he grinned. "Oh good. You brought me the others."

12

FIERY FINDS

Edison pulled a potion out of his inventory and held it in one hand while clutching his sword in the other. "Tell us where you put our friends," he demanded.

"Don't worry, you'll see them in a minute," Brett said as he grabbed a potion and splashed it on Amira and Edison.

The instant the potion splashed on his body, Edison felt as if he couldn't move. His sword fell to the ground along with the bottle of potion, which spilled. Edison had never felt this tired in his whole life. Amira dropped her sword on the ground too. They stood silently, without an ounce of energy to battle Brett or Wayne.

Brett then splashed a potion that revived Amira and Edison, and he led them deeper into the cave. "See?" said Brett. "I make the most powerful potions in the Overworld."

At the end of the cave there was an ice door, and Brett opened it.

"Edison!" Billy shouted.

"Amira!" Anna called out.

"Run!" Billy ordered his friends.

Edison knew running was pointless because Brett held the potion of weakness next to them, and the minute they tried to run off, he'd splash them and they'd lack any energy. Edison and Amira joined their friends in the icy prison. Brett laughed as he closed the door.

Through the ice door, they could hear Brett say to Wayne, "Now that we don't have to worry about them, we can stage an epic attack on Verdant Valley and Farmer's Bay, and the Alchemist Olympics will be canceled."

Edison stood by the door and listened to Wayne and Brett talk, but there was nothing he could do. He felt helpless.

Billy stood next to Edison. "We have to do something."

"They have my sword. I don't have another one in my inventory." Amira searched her inventory, which was almost empty.

Edison looked through his inventory. He had luckily put an extra sword in there, but it was the only one he had left. "I would give you one, but I only have one left."

Nobody else had an extra sword, and they worried that Amira would be incredibly vulnerable if they tried to attack without a sword. Anna said, "Even though

Amira doesn't have a sword, we still have to figure out how to escape. We can't stay trapped in here forever."

"I'm cold, it's freezing." Billy had the chills from the cold weather. "And we don't want them to destroy the contest."

"I can't believe Wayne and Brett were working together," said Amira.

"I know," said Edison. "They really fooled us."

Billy, Edison, and Amira talked over their options as they tried to make sense of the situation, but Anna didn't join in the conversation. She just looked through her inventory and tried to find obsidian, flint, and the other ingredients necessary to craft a portal to the Nether.

"Anna, what do you think?" asked Billy.

"Think about what? I wasn't listening," she confessed.

"Were we wrong to listen to Wayne?" Billy was annoyed. He had no idea why Anna wasn't listening, and he hated repeating himself.

Anna didn't respond to Billy. Instead she kept searching through her inventory.

"What are you looking for?" Amira asked Anna.

"I have an idea. A way to get us out of here," she announced.

"What?" asked Edison.

"I just need another obsidian block," Anna told them.

"You want us to build a portal to the Nether?" asked Edison.

"That's a fantastic idea." Billy pulled an obsidian block from his inventory. "Let's build it now."

"Before we do," Edison said, "I just want to make sure Amira will be okay in such an inhospitable environment." He looked at Amira. "Do you have a bow and arrow in your inventory?"

"Or snowballs?" added Anna.

Amira's inventory was low, but she did have three snowballs and a bow and arrow. She nodded her head.

"Great! Then you should be okay," said Anna.

The gang silently crafted a portal to the Nether. As they stood together on the small platform, purple mist enveloped them, and Edison wondered if the mist would seep underneath the doorway and alert Wayne and Brett to their plan. He stared at the icy door, but it never opened. Seconds later, they were in the hot Nether, and the chills they had felt in the icy prison were just a distant memory.

Ghasts flew by them, shooting fireballs at the group. Amira grabbed her bow and arrow.

"Don't waste any arrows!" advised Edison. "Use your fists."

Amira was out of sorts in the Nether because she spent most of her time on a boat and rarely traveled to this hot biome. As the fireball flew toward her, she didn't want to use her fists, because she was afraid she'd burn her hands. Instead she ducked away from the fireball and shot an arrow at the ghast, which hit the white flying menace and destroyed it.

"Don't waste your arrows," Anna said. "You're going to need them."

Amira watched Anna fearlessly punch the fireball with her fist. The fireball flew back at the ghast, obliterating it.

Anna and Amira picked up the dropped ghast tears and handed them to Edison. "We want you to use these in the competition."

Edison hoped the competition would go on. "Thank you," he said with a smile.

Billy pointed to a Nether fortress in the distance. He was a treasure hunter, and he was drawn to any stop where he had the potential to find riches. "Guys, we should go to that Nether fortress."

"We can't. We have to build another portal back to the Overworld," said Edison. Two zombie pigmen walked by them. "There's no point sticking around here. There is a competition to save."

"But you can find netherrack and Nether wart for your potions." Billy knew that it would be tough to convince the gang to travel to the Nether fortress, but he was still going to try.

The others agreed. But as they searched through their inventories for the tools to build the portal, a swarm of blazes flew toward them, showering the gang with fireballs.

Edison slammed the fiery fiends with snowballs, but he quickly ran out. "Snowballs!" cried Edison. "I need more snowballs." But there wasn't time to replenish his supply. Three fireballs struck him, leaving him with onc hcart. He tried to dodge a fireball that flew directly at him, but the hot ball landed on his leg, and Edison awoke in a cold igloo.

13

COLD

Edison awoke in the igloo. His feet were cold, and he was alone. Sitting up in bed, he searched through his inventory for an apple or anything to help him get his energy back. He found a potato, which he ate slowly, savoring each bite. He was freezing, and his legs shook as he swallowed his last piece of the potato. In the stillness of the wintery world, Edison could hear voices in the distance. Edison couldn't make out the sound of the voices, but if they belonged to Wayne and Brett, he didn't want them to see him. Searching through his inventory, he found a potion of invisibility and doused himself. When the potion made him invisible, he went outside to investigate.

Snow fell from the sky, blanketing the ground with a fresh layer. Despite the harsh chill, the biome was very peaceful. Edison walked around the frosty biome searching for the voices he had heard earlier, but there was nobody there. He knew this potion wasn't going to last much longer, and he dashed to the cave to see if Wayne and Brett were still there, plotting to end the competition. He walked deeper into the cave, opening the icy door to the prison, but it was empty.

Edison knew he only had a few seconds left before the potion wore off, and he sped out of the cave. He wanted to cover as much ground as he could in the wintery wonderland, but there seemed to be nobody in sight. Edison looked in every crevice of the biome, searching in another cave and behind the igloo, but he couldn't find the people whom he had heard earlier.

As Edison became visible, he heard a voice call out to him. "Edison." The familiar voice was loud but it sounded weak. He turned around and spotted Amira clinging to the doorway of the igloo.

"Edison." Her voice was growing faint and shaky. "I need your help. I don't have any energy, and my inventory is empty."

Edison hurried to Amira and handed her a potion of instant health. She drank it quickly, and her health bar was refreshed.

"Thank you." Amira smiled. "I was destroyed by a wither skeleton."

Edison knew that you usually found wither skeletons in the Nether fortress and asked, "You guys went into the Nether fortress?"

"We had to go there. It was the only way to escape the blaze invasion. There were so many of them. Of course once we were in the Nether fortress, we had another group of beasts to deal with, and I was destroyed. The plus side is Billy found Nether wart for you, so you can use it to brew potions, which we thought would make you happy."

"Happy?" Edison seemed confused. "How would that make me happy?"

"Because you're an alchemist."

Edison spoke very quickly. "It's funny, because all I ever wanted to do was brew potions, but now I just want to save everyone from Wayne and Brett. I don't understand how people can be so mean and want to destroy a fun activity like a brewing competition."

"I don't know either," remarked Amira, "but I will do everything I can to stop them."

A voice called out from behind them, "You will?"

Wayne and Brett stood side by side. They looked like twins, and it was hard to tell them apart. Edison studied their faces and could tell the difference by their eye color. Wayne had dark eyes, and Brett had light ones.

"How do you plan on stopping us?" Brett asked with a laugh.

Amira knew her inventory was empty and she had no way to attack them, and Edison only had a few items left. However, they weren't going to reveal their incredible disadvantage. Instead, Edison took out his last bottle of potion of weakness and poured it on Wayne and Brett. The duo became frozen and weak, and Edison considered destroying them with his diamond sword, but he wasn't sure where they'd respawn.

The snow covered Amira's dark hair, and she pushed the hair from her eyes as she pulled out her bow. Then she realized she didn't have any arrows.

Wayne laughed. Edison put his sword up to Wayne's back. "This isn't funny."

"How are you going to attack us? Amira doesn't even have any arrows left," Wayne said with a chuckle.

Edison pierced Wayne's back with the sword and he cried out in pain. Edison then handed arrows to Amira.

Amira aimed at Wayne. The arrows ripped through his arm. His health was diminishing. Before Amira shot an arrow at Brett, Edison said to the two criminals, "You're coming with us. Start climbing up the mountain."

The potion of weakness had worn off, and even though Wayne had been struck by the sword and arrow, he had enough energy to laugh as he splashed a potion of invisibility on himself and Brett, and they were gone.

"Don't worry about them," said Amira. "We have to get back to Verdant Valley. We will get them, I promise."

Edison focused on the words *I promise.* He had made a promise to Luna that he'd make sure the Alchemist Olympics would take place, despite knowing it was an almost impossible promise. Now he heard Amira making a similar promise. She wanted to stop Wayne and Brett, but she and Edison both knew this would be a promise they were going to have to work really hard to keep. As they climbed up the snow-covered mountain toward Verdant Valley, they tried to remain positive.

"Once we get back to Verdant Valley, I'm sure we'll be reunited with Billy and Anna," said Edison.

"I bet you're right," said Amira.

"We have to come up with a really good plan," said Edison. "The competition is just a few days away, and we have to stop them so it can go on."

Edison didn't focus on the fact that if the competition did take place, he wasn't prepared for it. He wasn't able to practice because he had spent so much time trying to save the competition. Instead, he just focused on various ways to stop Wayne and Brett. These thoughts spun around in his head. He was overwhelmed with many ideas, but he didn't have one solid plan, and this worried him. He wished he had the perfect plan, but he didn't.

Silently they trekked down the mountain, watching that they didn't slip on the icy ground. They were both immersed in thought, trying to come up with a plan to help save the Alchemist Olympics and punish Wayne and Brett.

They finally reached the bottom of the mountain. "Don't worry." Amira's voice was strong when she spoke. "I have a plan."

14

COUNTDOWN TO THE COMPETITION

"What is it?" Edison asked as they walked down the mountain.

"Since it's just a few days until the competition, we know Wayne and Brett are going to show up. We have to get the entire crew from the competition and all of our friends and neighbors to help us beat them."

Edison thought that Amira's plan sounded too easy, but he didn't want to tell her because it might make Amira feel bad. He believed once they told the others that they needed their help, Luna would cancel the competition. He understood that Luna didn't want to risk harming anyone because of these attacks, and she would rather stop the competition than let people get injured. He also knew if they didn't return to Verdant Valley, Amira wouldn't be able to survive. She had nothing in her inventory and needed to get back to her mammoth ship where she stored all of her supplies.

Verdant Valley was in sight, and they hurried to reach the center of town. When they got closer, they could hear Billy call out to them. Edison smiled when he heard his friend's voice.

"You guys are back," Billy said breathlessly while running over to them.

"Yes," Amira said, "but my inventory is empty. I have to get back to my ship."

"What is going on here?" asked Edison.

"There hasn't been an attack since we left," Billy smiled.

"Wow, that's great. "What about the competition?" Edison asked.

"Since there haven't been any attacks, Luna said the competition could go on. It starts in two days. I think we should head back to your place and start to prepare," said Billy.

"Now that we've figured out why the potion of invisibility was so strong, you should be fine," said Amira.

"I will time you," said Billy.

Edison didn't feel as optimistic as the others. Even though there hadn't been an attack in a few days, it didn't mean everything was okay. "What about Brett and Wayne? They must be planning something huge. I don't think Luna should let the Alchemist Olympics happen."

"When Brett and Wayne come back, they will be

outnumbered. It will be okay. We know they are behind this, and that gives us an advantage," said Amira.

"I'd feel much better if we postponed the competition for a few days and I could go find Brett and Wayne and make sure they aren't a threat. I'm going to speak to Luna about it," said Edison.

"Okay," said Billy, "But I'm not sure she will allow the competition to be rescheduled. There are a lot of people coming to town in the next two days, and they'll want to go to the Alchemist Olympics when they arrive."

"We have to take everyone's safety into account." Edison couldn't believe he had to explain this to his friends. Didn't they understand that Wayne and Brett were targeting the competition?

Edison spotted Luna in the distance and hurried toward her. He quickly explained all of the reasons she needed to postpone the competition. She listened, and before she could speak, thunder shook the grassy ground in Verdant Valley and rain began to fall. Edison and the others followed Luna, who was already running toward the castle to get shelter from this unexpected rainstorm. The sound of clanging bones rattled through the area.

Omar, who was busy putting the finishing details on the stage when the rain started, suddenly found himself surrounded by four skeletons. "Help!" he cried.

Amira turned around and wanted to run to her friend who stood by the stage, but she remembered her inventory was bare. She had no way of helping him.

She spotted Anna's purple hair near the entrance to the castle.

"Anna," Amira called out, "you have to help Omar. He's surrounded by skeletons near the stage, and I don't have anything in my inventory."

Anna, dressed in full armor, came charging out of the castle toward Omar, clutching an enchanted diamond sword as she struck the skeletons that attacked him. Together they were able to annihilate the skeletons, but more began marching through the town.

"Did Wayne and Brett spawn a storm?" asked Anna as the rain fell and she raced with Omar through puddles to join their friends in the castle.

When they entered the castle, they were relieved to see that it was free from skeletons. It was filled with people wearing armor and drinking potions for strength. They were getting ready to battle the skeletons that seemed to continuously spawn in the rainy town.

"I don't think we should keep the competition going," said Luna.

Edison surprised Amira and Billy when he said, "We should. We know who is behind this attack, and we will stop them. Maybe we have to postpone it a few days, but people have worked very hard to prepare for this competition, and it wouldn't be fair if we let Wayne and Brett destroy it."

Luna said, "I agree. Edison, we won't stop this competition because of these bullies. We will work with you guys to stop the attacks."

Knowing that he had the entire team from the Alchemist Olympics on his side made Edison confident they would win this battle. Dressed in diamond armor, the group raced into the skeleton invasion and began to battle. Before they had a chance to destroy a skeleton, the sun started to shine.

Edison walked over to Luna. "Now that we have a break from this battle, I think we should put together a team to find Brett and Wayne."

"That's a good idea." Luna looked at her group and asked for volunteers to help find Wayne and Brett."

As people gathered to join Edison in his mission to end the attacks, a large three-headed beast spawned in the skies above them.

"Oh no!" Luna cried, "They spawned a Wither."

"We have to stop it," Edison declared, knowing a battle against the Wither would be no easy task. Wayne and Brett were trying hard to weaken them and stop the competition.

The Wither was blue, but as it morphed into another color, there was a loud explosion.

"Amira!" Edison called out as he watched his friend and others destroyed by the explosion.

Edison knew she'd respawn in the Cold Taiga Biome, and he hoped she'd teleport back to Verdant Valley, but he didn't have time to think about Amira, because the Wither was shooting skulls at him. In the grassy Verdant Valley, there were few places to hide from this flying terror. The beast spit skulls at the group and successfully destroyed a number of people from the Alchemist Olympic group.

"How are we going to destroy this mob boss?" asked Billy.

Edison looked up at the sky. He needed to come up with a plan, and he needed to do it now.

15

WITHER ATTACK

The skulls shot out of the Wither's three heads and onto the people in the middle of Verdant Valley. Edison saw Anna shielding herself with the door to her home as she shot arrows at the Wither. He joined her. The Wither weakened with each arrow that landed in its black flesh. Edison stared at the beast's gray eyes as it shot a blue skull at them. A trail of smoke flew through the sky as the skull approached him. He shot the skull with an arrow, destroying it.

"The blue ones are slower," said Anna, "but I can't handle the black skulls. They are so powerful."

As she spoke, the Wither spit out two black skulls. The sky was filled with smoke as the skulls flew at them. Edison and Anna ran into the house, but the skulls landed on the door.

"My door is gone." Anna raced to the entryway, but

more skulls were flying in their direction and she had to bolt back into the living room.

"We have to find a way to stop this Wither," said Edison. "I wonder where Wayne and Brett built the spawner for it."

"We can't look for it. We just have to destroy this beast." As Anna spoke, she rushed to the entryway to hit the Wither with an arrow, but she was struck by a black smoky skull that flew through the opening. She was incredibly weak—her body was reacting to the Wither effect. Edison watched in horror as her hearts turned black.

Edison handed Anna a cup of milk. As she sipped the milk, her health bar was replenished.

"The armor doesn't even help," Anna said. She finished the milk. "This is an incredibly difficult enemy. I don't know how we'll survive."

Without the door to shield them from the Wither, they were left exposed and vulnerable. They were about to race toward the Wither to attack it when they heard a voice call out, "Edison! Anna!" Amira had teleported into the living room. The gang ran to greet their friend.

"Amira," Edison asked, "are you okay?"

"My inventory is still empty," she replied.

"You can't stay near the door," Anna explained. "A wither skull destroyed it, and it's too dangerous."

"You need supplies," Edison said.

Anna rushed into her bedroom and brought a large chest into the living room. She lifted the cover of the chest. Gold armor glistened, and a diamond sword rested underneath the armor. "Take what you need," she said to Amira and raced back to the open doorway.

Using her bow and arrow, Anna struck the Wither with another arrow into one of the three heads.

Edison hurried out of the house and was shocked to see the town of Verdant Valley completely empty. The Wither narrowed its focus on him as he tried to hide behind trees or anything to avoid being struck by the barrage of wither skulls.

The skulls shot down and one landed on his exposed arm. He was struck with the Wither effect and had little energy. He couldn't even muster up the strength to get the milk from his inventory. His hearts were black, and there was nobody to help him. He heard a voice as he stood alone, hoping he wouldn't be struck by another skull.

"Over here," Omar called out from behind the stage.

Edison didn't move, and Omar didn't understand his friend's reaction and called out again, "Edison, what's the matter? Come here!"

Still Edison was too weak to reply.

Omar rushed over to Edison, trying to dodge the skulls that shot down from the sky. As he got closer he saw Edison's dark hearts. "Oh no! You've been struck." He handed Edison a potion to regain his strength.

Edison said to Omar, "We have to destroy this beast."

"I know," said Omar. "Come to the stage."

Edison regained his strength and followed Omar to the stage.

Behind the stage were a group of people holding bows and arrows, and Edison was relieved when he saw Billy.

"We have a plan," Billy told him. "Just follow us."

Omar called out, "Now!"

The group stood up and shot a wave of arrows at the Wither, destroying the flying menace.

The Wither exploded, and a lone Nether star dropped from the sky, landing in the center of Verdant Valley.

"You should take it, Omar," suggested Billy. "This was your plan."

The rest of the group agreed. Omar leaned down to pick it up as Anna and Amira joined them.

Luna rushed toward the group. "We only have a short time before people start arriving for the competition."

"We have to find Wayne and Brett," said Edison.

"They can't be far from here, because they spawned the Wither," said Omar.

A voice boomed through the town: "We're a lot closer than you think."

16
MISSED OPPORTUNITIES

"It's over, Wayne," Edison called out.

"Really? It is?" Wayne asked with a chuckle.

The group that had clustered behind the stage rushed toward Wayne and Brett, but they were unable to capture the tricky duo. Wayne and Brett splashed a potion on anyone who got within a few inches of them, making everyone invisible and weak.

"What's going on?" questioned Omar. All of his energy was drained, and he had disappeared.

"Oh no," Edison explained, his voice growing weaker with each breath. "They splashed us with the potion of invisibility that was tainted. It's very strong. I don't even know what happens to me when I take it. I—" Edison disappeared before he could finish the sentence. When the potion wore off, he found himself in the center of Verdant Valley, but he was alone. There weren't any people in sight, and Edison waited to see if they'd respawn. It felt like he was waiting forever, and he was still alone.

Edison leaned against the edge of the stage. He was extremely woozy and grabbed a potion of instant strength from his inventory and drank it. With renewed energy he ran into the castle, looking for anyone at all. His heart sunk as he searched through each room, but they were all empty. As Edison exited the castle, he could hear muffled voices.

"Is someone there?" he called out.

There was no response.

"I can help you," Edison said, but there was just silence. He didn't hear the muffled voices again. Then he heard the rattling of bones. Hiding behind a door, he watched as a gang of skeletons searched the castle. Despite trying to shield himself behind the door, one of the skeletons spotted Edison and shot an arrow at him. The arrow ripped through Edison's arm, stinging him. "Ouch!" he cried as he leaped at the skeleton with his diamond sword.

His sword landed on the skeleton, but Edison couldn't celebrate the small victory because two more arrows had pierced his other arm. He was losing hearts quickly, and he needed help, but there was nobody in sight. Edison tried to ignore the pain in his arms, as he pulled a potion from his inventory and splashed it on the skeletons.

The potion weakened the bony beasts, and Edison swung his sword at them, trying to annihilate the skeletons before they destroyed him. He had obliterated two skeletons, leaving their dropped bones on the ground. He leaped at the last skeleton when he could hear more rattling bones in the distance. Edison slammed his sword against the skeleton's bony body, destroying the final skeleton. He quickly picked up the bones from the ground and placed them in his inventory. He searched for a powerful potion that he could splash on the skeletons that were invading the castle. Readjusting his armor, he fearlessly raced toward the sound of the bones. He had to accept his fate. If he sat and waited for them to destroy him, he'd simply be wasting valuable time. He must end this battle and find his friends. He also had to stop Wayne and Brett, who appeared almost unstoppable. In his short life as a detective, he had never encountered such tough criminals. He needed his friends to help him capture Wayne and Brett.

Edison lunged toward the skeletons but gasped when he saw what appeared to be over twenty skeletons crowding the hall of the castle. His first instinct was to run from the bony beasts, but they had spotted him and aimed their arrows at his unarmored arms. Even if he had a full health bar and hearts, he wouldn't be able to withstand an attack of this magnitude. He feared he'd respawn in the igloo. His heart beat rapidly as he tried to dodge the arrows while rushing toward the skeletons.

"Edison!" Billy called out.

Edison couldn't turn around. "What?"

"Get out of the way!" Billy hollered.

Edison ducked into a room off the hallway and looked for Billy. He was relieved when he saw Billy,

Anna, Amira, Omar, Luna, Peyton, and Erin dashing down the hall with their swords. Edison rushed to join his friends in battle, and they slew the skeletons within seconds.

"Where are Wayne and Brett?" asked Edison.

"We thought you were going to find them," said Omar.

"Aren't you the detective?" questioned Luna.

Edison heard the sound of more skeletons marching into the castle. Omar suggested they put up the bridge so the skeletons couldn't cross over the moat.

"Good idea," remarked Luna. "Amira, put up the bridge, and we'll battle the skeletons that are already here."

Edison said, "And I will find Wayne and Brett."

Billy looked at Edison. "I will go with you."

"Me too," said Anna.

"You guys are going to stop Wayne and Brett? What about the bridge?" asked Luna as she clutched her sword and prepared to battle the skeletons that were advancing toward them.

"I'll put the bridge up, and they can find Wayne and Brett," said Amira.

"I promise we will stop them," Edison said, and he knew this was one promise he was determined to keep. "And I know the first place we should look for them."

17

ULTIMATE TRUST

"I can't believe they're actually here," Edison said as he clutched a bottle of potion. "It seems almost too easy."

"Maybe it's a trap," Anna whispered in his ear.

They hid behind the dirt entrance to the cave outside of Verdant Valley as they watched Wayne and Brett construct a skeleton spawner.

"What should we do?" asked Billy. "Should we surprise them?"

"Yes, but we have to be careful. They have that incredibly powerful potion, which seems to have grown stronger."

"Yeah," Anna agreed. "Last time he splashed it on all of us, we wound up waking up in the other part of town."

"Yes," said Billy. "They are crafting very potent potions. I think we have to keep our distance."

"Maybe we should attack them with arrows?" suggested Anna.

The group agreed that arrows were the best method of attack, so they picked up bows and arrows from their inventories and tore into the cave. The barrage of arrows struck Wayne's and Brett's unarmored bodies. Wayne fell back and was unable to put the finishing touches on the skeleton spawner. The surprise attack weakened the duo.

"This is over," Edison yelled as he shot more arrows at the redheaded terrors.

"Never!" shouted Brett.

Wayne pulled out a bottle of potion from his inventory, but Edison's arrows struck the glass bottle and it shattered. The contents dripped to the floor. Wayne reached into his inventory for another bottle, but there wasn't another one. "Brett?" He looked at his friend.

Brett reached into his inventory, but two arrows landed on his chest, and he was left with one heart. He used his last bit of strength to reach for a bottle, but his inventory was also empty.

"Brett, come on!" Wayne yelled.

Brett dodged an arrow as he said, "I am done with you. I am done with this attack. You've failed me, Wayne."

"Me? I failed you?" Wayne shouted.

"This was all your idea. You tainted the gold bars with command blocks," said Brett.

"You told me to do that," said Wayne.

Edison, Billy, and Anna stopped shooting arrows.

They knew that Wayne and Brett had only one heart left each, and they didn't want to destroy them, which would allow the tricksters to respawn in another location and get away. Besides, they liked watching Wayne and Brett bicker. Edison and the gang knew that if you weren't aligned with your partner, you could jeopardize your goal. It appeared that their plan to destroy the Alchemist Olympics was quickly fading.

"Let's get this criminal." Wayne pointed at Brett.

Edison walked deeper into the cave. He still kept a safe distance because he was worried this might be a trap. Perhaps the devious pair did have potions in their inventories and would attack the gang.

Edison spoke. "For the past month, all I have done was work to make sure I was prepared for the competition. Two of my good friends even came to town to see me participate in it. In fact, from the day I received the letter that I'd be in the brewing competition, I was happy and excited. It was literally a dream come true for me, but then you come here and cause all of this trouble and try to stop the competition, and I just want to know why. Why are you so intent on ruining a competition that we all have worked so hard to be a part of? Why do you want to destroy other people's happiness?"

There was silence.

"They don't even have a response," Anna remarked.

Billy aimed his bow and arrow. "You guys are coming with us."

Wayne and Brett looked at the ground as they walked toward the group. When they reached the exit, the sun was setting.

"We have to get back to town before dark," ordered Edison, "so we have to walk faster."

As they approached Verdant Valley with Wayne and Brett, Amira rushed over with the news. "We were able to deactivate the spawner in the old mineshaft. They had placed a new one there."

"Are there any more spawners?" asked Edison.

"No," Brett replied.

"Well, we will find out if you're telling the truth soon enough," Edison said.

Luna rushed out of the castle. "You found them! Good job!"

Edison, Billy, and Anna blushed. They didn't like the attention when they solved a case, but they loved helping people. Of course, this case had special importance to Edison, and he'd have the ultimate reward at the end.

"Now that you found the two culprits behind these attacks, we can place them in a safe place and keep an eye on them, and we can start planning for the competition. People should be arriving in town soon."

Edison was excited, but he also wanted answers from Wayne and Brett. As they escorted them toward a bedrock room in the castle he asked, "Please tell me why you did this. I have to know."

Wayne said, "We are the best alchemists in the Overworld."

"And we weren't invited into the competition," added Brett.

"They said we were disqualified because we use potions that are tainted and because we use command blocks." Wayne was upset.

Luna responded, "The Alchemist Olympics is for the best alchemists. We want only those who follow the rules and brew potions with the proper ingredients."

Edison was annoyed. "Just because you didn't get in doesn't mean you have to ruin it for the rest of us."

"I know that now"—Wayne looked at Edison—"and we're sorry. Can you let us go?"

"We can't let you go," said Luna.

"Why not?" Brett pleaded.

"I can't believe you even have to ask us this question." Luna didn't really want to bother crafting a response, but the criminals had to know why they were being held prisoner.

Edison said, "We don't trust you."

"That's one reason," said Luna, "among many."

Wayne said, "You don't have to list the reasons. I know what we did was unforgivable, and I will accept our punishment."

"I wouldn't say it's unforgivable, but I do want you to understand how much you've impacted the competition. We are behind schedule, and you almost had the event canceled," explained Luna.

Omar nudged Wayne and Brett into the bedrock room. "I will keep an eye on them, and you should get ready for the competition. I will make sure they are secure." Omar looked at Edison. "And don't worry, Edison. I will be there when you win a medal."

Edison didn't think he was going to win a medal, but he was just glad the case had been solved and the competition would go on. He was happy that the alchemists from around the Overworld who were arriving at Verdant Valley that night would be able to participate and win whatever medal they deserved.

Edison walked into the bedrock room where Wayne and Brett were going to be held. "I'm glad you didn't ruin the competition. You guys can stay in here and think about what you have done."

"I really wanted to be your friend," Wayne said. "I'm sorry."

Edison let the words *I'm sorry* sink in. He didn't respond, but he left knowing that his words and actions made a difference.

"People are arriving," a woman in an Alchemist Olympics shirt called out. "We have to go prepare for the opening ceremony."

Luna quickly joined the woman, ready to start the competition. Billy called out to Edison, "Do you think we have a few more minutes to practice before the event begins?"

"I hope so." Edison smiled at his friend, and they hurried back to Edison's bungalow in Farmer's Bay to do one last practice brewing session before packing up all of the belongings he needed to bring to the Alchemist Olympics.

18

BREWING

The competition was about to begin and crowds formed by the stage. Edison enjoyed watching the Alchemist Olympics events until he realized that the brewing competition was about to begin. When Edison's name was called and he stepped up onto the stage, his heart began to race. He took a deep breath to calm himself, but it didn't help.

Edison had never brewed in front of a crowd, so he was nervous as he stood on stage and began to make the potion of invisibility. He took out the ingredients and looked at the brewing station. Although these items were very familiar to him, they didn't offer him comfort as he heard the voices from the crowd. How was he going to brew potions that were worthy of an award while people watched? He worried that the crowd would be too distracting for him, but he told himself that if he just concentrated on the brewing, he'd be okay. He reminded himself that he had just battled two ultimate menaces and he had helped the Alchemist Olympics go on, and that he should have more confidence.

Slowly Edison added the fermented spider eye into the potion of night vision, and sipped. His heart beat fast as he hoped it wasn't a tainted batch. Edison quickly became invisible while he watched the judge time him and the others. The four other participants disappeared at the same time but reappeared while Edison was still invisible. Edison was the last to reappear.

"Edison. You are the winner," said the judge.

Edison was shocked. He couldn't believe he'd won. He was so excited to win the medal, but what made him even happier was seeing Omar's and Amira's smiling faces in the crowd. They appeared even happier than he was. He knew he would cherish this medal and this moment.

"The competition is over," Luna announced.

People rushed to the large celebration on the castle lawn, but Edison didn't join them. He could hear Anna and Billy calling out to him, but he excused himself and surprised everyone when he went to see Wayne and Brett after making a quick stop at the party. He brought them each a slice of cake from the celebration.

Wayne smiled. "Thanks." He was surprised at this act of kindness.

Brett gobbled up the cake, and with a mouth full of food said, "This was very nice of you."

Wayne pointed to the medal on Edison's gray T-shirt. "I see you won a medal."

"Yes," Edison said, "and maybe one day you guys can win one too. I'm sure you're great alchemists."

"But we cheated," confessed Wayne.

"I bet if you stopped cheating, you'd realize you're just as good as the rest of us," said Edison.

Edison left the two with those parting words as he walked back to the party. He could hear music and people laughing in the distance. As he got closer to the party, Billy jogged toward Edison. "Are you back? We have to celebrate."

"Yes." Edison spotted Anna's purple hair in the crowd, and they walked over to her. "It looks like we successfully solved another case."

"Yes," Anna said with a smile.

"I hope it's our last case," Edison confessed. He wanted to get back to his life of alchemy. It had been a while since he had worked at the potion stand in Farmer's Bay.

"I'm sure it isn't," said Billy.

"We have to help people if they come to us in need," said Anna.

As Edison feasted on cake and cookies, he soaked in the laughter and music at the party and gazed happily at his medal. He didn't get a medal for solving the problems in the Overworld, but he had the same feeling of satisfaction, and that was all he needed.

The End

WANT TO READ ABOUT STEVIE AND HIS FRIENDS?

Read the Unofficial Overworld Adventure series!

Escape from the
Overworld
DANICA DAVIDSON

Attack on the
Overworld
DANICA DAVIDSON

The Rise of
Herobrine
DANICA DAVIDSON

Down into the
Nether
DANICA DAVIDSON

The Armies of
Herobrine
DANICA DAVIDSON

Battle with the
Wither
DANICA DAVIDSON

Available wherever books are sold!

DO YOU LIKE FICTION FOR MINECRAFTERS?

Read the Unofficial Minecrafters Academy series!

Zombie Invasion
WINTER MORGAN

Skeleton Battle
WINTER MORGAN

Battle in the Overworld
WINTER MORGAN

Attack on Minecrafters Academy
WINTER MORGAN

Hidden in the Chest
WINTER MORGAN

Encounters in End City
WINTER MORGAN